S0-CWR-797

10/18/00

To Jackie -
A good story is like a rolling
stone. It picks up speed and
knocks you off your feet!

♡ Alypia
Gonzalez

10/18/00

AG

Special thanks to Alysia,
Sherry, Lisa, Lavaille, Kathryn,
& all my librarian friends who helped me out

And also to Mom and Dad,
Seumean, Muoy, and Leng for being
the best family I could ever ask for...

In His Glory,
V.K.

Text copyright © 2000 by Providence Publishing
Illustrations copyright © 2000 by Providence Publishing
All rights reserved.
Published by Providence Publishing (888)966-3833
1317 Ben Hur, Houston, TX 77055
& Hajimzel Publishing (281) 498-8120
12600 Bissonnet, Ste. A455, Houston, TX 77099
Printed in Hong Kong by Creative Printing USA
First Printing 10 9 8 7 6 5 4 3 2

Library of Congress Catalog Card Number 99-075879
Kimmel, Eric; Kuon, Vuthy, The Rolling Stone & Other Read-Aloud Stories
Summary: An anthology of children's read-aloud stories
ISBN 0-9651661-2-0

The Rolling Stone

& other Read-Aloud Stories

FEATURE STORY WRITTEN BY **ERIC KIMMEL**

FEATURE STORY ILLUSTRATED BY **VUTHY KUON**

EDITED BY **ALYSIA GONZALEZ**

HAJIMZEL • PROVIDENCE

Table of Contents

The Rolling Stone

by Eric A. Kimmel

A big stone once stood halfway up the hill overlooking the town of Chelm. The stone's location had been bothering the people of Chelm for generations. All agreed it didn't belong where it was. Some thought a stone of that size ought to be at the top of the hill. Others thought it should be at the bottom of the hill.

One day the mayor said, "Let's settle this stone business once and for all. We'll climb the hill to the stone. Those who think the stone should be at the top of the hill will push up. Those who think it should be at the bottom of the hill will push down. Whoever pushes hardest, wins."

The people of Chelm thought this was a fine idea. They climbed the hill and began pushing. Half pushed up; half pushed down. The stone stayed where it was.

A traveler came riding by. He saw all the people on the hill pushing at the stone. "What are you doing?" he asked them.

"We're trying to decide once and for all where this stone should be."

"Why not let the stone decide?" the man said. He walked up the hill, gave the stone a push sideways, and watched it roll. It rolled all the way to the bottom of the hill.

"Aha!" the people cried. "So that's where the stone wants to be!"

And there it sits, at the bottom of the hill, to this day.

The Magician's Spell

by Brekka Hervey

Once upon a time, a young and lazy prince named Pepperdine was learning the ways of magic from his father's most powerful magician. He was an inept student and rarely paid heed to the magician's commands. The magician, whose temper was as short as his magic was strong, became so angry when the prince did not complete his studies that he placed a spell on the boy.

From that day forward, the prince was forced to carry with him always a magical book and quill pen. Each morning at sunrise, the book opened, and the prince was forced to work for hours writing. Only when the book was satisfied with Prince Pepperdine's words did it finally slam shut. Resentment toward the magician filled the lazy prince.

Years passed, yet the book's pages never seemed to fill. The young prince grew to be a man, and his father grew old. As the king's health failed, Pepperdine was forced to take on more of the responsibilities for running the kingdom, but sighed bitterly as he took no joy in doing so.

One day, a neighboring warrior, angry and powerful, entered the kingdom. Word spread that the warrior planned to make the kingdom his own. The prince's advisors begged him to take action quickly lest the kingdom be lost, yet the prince cowered in his palace.

As the prince was writing in his book one morning, the warrior came and demanded to see him. "I have heard," said he, "that you are as lazy as your father is old. Give up your kingdom, and I shall not kill you." The prince's pen trembled in his hands.

Then, looking at his book, a thought came to him. "Are you challenging me to a duel? Then it is my right to choose the weapon," said Pepperdine. "I choose the pen."

The warrior frowned, yet due to the rules of chivalry, he had no choice but to concede. "The first man to convince the other of his superiority as a ruler will win the kingdom," said the prince, setting his book between them. They both took their stance, each with pen in hand. The warrior attacked. The pen whipped through the air! The ink splashed! The pages filled.

Prince Pepperdine counter-attacked using powerful arguments, elaborate explanations, and immaculate grammar. For hours they took turns writing, and before the the sun had set, the powerful warrior, void of ideas, became exhausted. Sorely defeated, he fled. The prince's advisors gathered around. "You have saved the kingdom!" they cried. "All hail Prince Pepperdine!"

The prince knew he could never have triumphed without the help of his childhood teacher, so he set out to find the magician and thank him. And when he did, his teacher said to him, "You have done well. Your hard work has paid off. So from this day forward, the spell is forever broken."

The next morning, for the first time, he awoke to see the book unopened. He took up his pen, opened the book and began to write. That morning, and every morning thereafter, the prince wrote joyfully. Thus, Prince Pepperdine became a goodly king, just and industrious. Even now, the book is a sacred relic in his kingdom, for it is filled with wisdom that knows no bounds.

The Girl & the Frog

by Lisa Jastram

Once upon a time, there was a girl whose best friend happened to be a frog. The two of them spent many happy hours together hopping around, swimming in the river and catching bugs.

One day, she thought she heard a voice whispering, "Kiss the frog." She looked around but saw no one.

"Why should I kiss the frog?" she demanded.

"Because he will turn into a handsome prince," the voice replied.

"And why should I want him to turn into a handsome prince?" she asked.

"Because," the voice said, "every girl needs a handsome prince."

"Maybe it's true," the girl thought to herself. "Maybe I do need a handsome prince." So she turned to her frog, puckered up her lips and... "SMACK!"

She opened her eyes and there before her stood a very handsome prince!

"Let's hop!" the girl said with excitement.

"Whatever for?" replied the prince. "I'd rather sit on my throne and order people about."

"Okay then," the girl said. "Let's go catch some bugs— maybe a mosquito or perhaps a gnat."

"Bugs?" cried out the prince with disgust. "Those nasty things? I think not. I'd much prefer having a cup of tea with a cucumber sandwich, perhaps."

"You will swim with me, won't you?" asked the girl.

"Swim? In that slimy river of yours?" the prince retorted. "Don't be absurd! How about a jolly good game of polo instead?"

"Polo? Cucumber sandwiches? Ordering people about?" exclaimed the girl. "Why you're no fun at all! I want my frog back!"

And even though it seemed a very disgusting thing to do, the girl took a deep breath, grabbed the prince and... "SMACK!"

There sat her best friend once again.

Off they happily hopped as the girl thought to herself, "I will never trade my good friend again— not even for a prince!"

Prince Adam

by Kendall Seuser

Once there was a little boy named Adam.

One day Adam said to his mother, "I want to be a prince with a castle, a moat, a drawbridge and lots of knights."

His mother said, "You will have to wait 'til tomorrow," as she kissed him and sent him to bed.

The next morning, Adam's mother called the rental store and ordered a backhoe, a bulldozer, and a dump truck. Several men, under the direction of Adam's mother, worked all day long digging a moat around Adam's house. As soon as the hole was dug, Adam's mother turned on her garden hose and filled the moat with water. Then Adam said, "Where's the castle?"

His mother said, "You will have to wait 'til tomorrow," as she kissed him and sent him to bed.

The next morning, Adam's mother called the rock quarry and ordered gray stones, mortar and bricks. Several men, under the direction of Adam's mother, worked all day long mortaring stone against stone, creating a large castle around Adam's house. As soon as the castle was finished, Adam's mother hung red banners around the castle. Then Adam said, "Where's the drawbridge?"

His mother said, "You will have to wait 'til tomorrow," as she kissed him and sent him to bed.

The next morning, Adam's mother called the lumber yard and ordered wood, chain, and nails. Several men, under the direction of Adam's mother, worked all day long hammering and nailing the giant drawbridge together. As soon as the bridge was made, Adam's mother walked over it into the castle. Then Adam said, "Where are the knights?"

His mother said, "You will have to wait 'til tomorrow," as she kissed him and sent him to bed.

The next morning, Adam's mother called the sheet metal plant and ordered sheets of metal, rivets, and strapping. Several men, under the direction of Adam's mother, worked all day long measuring, cutting, and transforming the sheet metal into suits of armor. As soon as the suits of armor were done, Adam's mother polished the metal with her best cleaning rag.

When everything was finished, Adam took his mother's hand and they walked to the top of the castle tower. Then Adam looked up at his mother, removed the crown from his own head and gently placed it on hers. He hugged his mother and said, "I love you."

As Adam looked around the castle with its moat, drawbridge, and knights, he saw the full moon in the dark night sky.

Then Adam said, "I think I'd like to be an astronaut!"

The Snake Song

by Lucas Miller

I went out one day in my garden, to water my corn and my beans.
I noticed a snake by my bare little toes, and I nearly jumped out of my jeans!

I yelled: EEK!! ACK!! HELP!! POLICE!! Please! I'm too young to die!
It's a wet, slimy snake with a flickering tongue, and a ravenous look in her eye!

I should've known that the snake wasn't slimy and known just to leave her alone.
She was more scared of me than I was of her and she slithered off under a stone.

I sure was relieved when she slithered away, and that, I can tell you, is true.
Now try to imagine that you are the snake-- can you see the snake's point of view?

I was s-s-slithering around in the garden, just tas-s-sting the air for a rat.
When a two-legged giant nearly s-s-stepped on me, and he just about s-s-squished me flat!
I thought, ZOIKS!! YIKES!! SLITHER FOR YOUR LIFE!! I'll bite if he doesn't move back.
That's one ugly monster. I better leave quick, or else he'll have me for a snack!

I peeked out again at my garden. My corn, it was sure looking dry.
When I checked things out, not a snake was in sight, so again I gave it a try.

Then I heard a rustle below me and saw an incredible sight.
A rat was there eating my corn, and that snake, it was ready to strike!

I said: YEAH!! RAD!! AWESOME!! COOL!! I'll tell you what we can do.
You keep on catching those troublesome rats, and I'll share my garden with you.

When YOU find a snake in your garden, it'll scare you down to your bones.
But there's no need to scream and there's no need to shout—
Just step back and leave 'em alone!

Elephants in Disguise

by Sherry Pearson

Once I knew an elephant who called herself a mouse.
She nibbled corn cheese oodles and she lived inside my house.
She hid behind the sofa where she slept throughout the day,
And every night she'd squeak, "Time for all good mice to play."

I could not understand it, how my parents never heard,
But when I tried to tell them, they would laugh, "Why, that's absurd!
Elephant knows it's elephant, as mouse knows it is mouse.
Indeed, if she existed, could she hide within our house?!"

So I saved the corn cheese oodles that my dad packed in my lunch,
I saved them for two weeks until I had a great, big bunch.
I set my watch for early. I woke up in the dark.
I bribed my dog with kibble and hoped he would not bark.

I scurried down the hallway, just as quiet as a mouse,
Or as quiet as the elephant who lives inside my house.
I went straight to the kitchen, found the light, and then was able
To see the mouse and elephant sitting on our dinner table.

Oh, they tried to run and hide, but I caught them by the tails,
"Please, wait! I will not hurt you and I promise not to tell.
If you'll answer all my questions, I promise you'll go free.
Besides, I've corn cheese oodles, and I'll share, if you'll agree."

They stared at one another and squeaked a mousy sigh,
"Ask us what you please, miss, for mice do not tell lies."
"But you are not a mouse," I said, addressing the elephant,
"You're bigger, wider, heavier, and you have that trunk in front."

"It's true, I was an elephant as was all my family,
My aunts and uncles, ancestors, since the eve of history.
But the world just keeps on changing as we always knew it would.
And we must change 'long with it or we'll all be gone for good.

There are men who hunt the elephant for their tusks of ivory,
I've seen it happen many times, with my friends and family.
The Old Ones held a council, and we listened to the wise,
For this was their solution, to be elephants in disguise.

So some pretend they're kittens, and some pretend they're cows,
We're all pretending something. As for me, well, I'm a mouse.
And people who love elephants, pretend along with us.
They hide us from the hunters who would kill us for our tusks."

The room grew quiet, quiet. I stared at the elephant's eyes.
I'd never noticed how small they were, about a mouse eye's size.
And the long, gray trunk was shrinking to a tiny, mousy nose,
And the giant, elephant pads became small, pink, mousy toes.

"You'd better hurry, scurry mice, your secret's safe with me,
But I just don't understand how my parents do not see."
"But they do," said ele... mouse. "They pretend well, don't you think?
For without imagination, elephants will be extinct."

"I have imagination, and I say you are a mouse,
But I think it's sad and lonely you must live inside a house."
"I hope it won't be too long that we elephants live apart.
Just keep pretending I'm a mouse, I'll be an elephant in my heart."

The Very Busy Bee

by Deanna Gonzales

There once was a busy bee named Beatrice. Beatrice was always busy. So busy, in fact, that she never took time to enjoy life. On any day of the week, Beatrice could be found buzzing from place to place, singing a quick hello and goodbye song as she passed her forest friends.

One fine morning as Beatrice hummed past Patty Parrot, she could be heard singing...

> Good morning, good morning, good morning, I'd love to talk to you.
> But I have so very many things that I have to do.
> I wish I could stay and chat some, I'd love to talk with you.
> But I must run and hang my clothes while the sky is still bright blue.

As Beatrice whirred along at a record pace, she passed Ricky Rabbit in his garden, gathering carrots to make his famous carrot stew.

> Good morning, good morning, good morning, I'd love to talk to you.
> But I have so very many things that I have to do.
> I wish I could stay and help you gather carrots for your stew.
> But today I'm in a hurry, the hours are so few.

And off she went, buzzing by as quickly as a bee could buzz, until she came upon her friend Bitsy Bird, lying beside the grand forest oak tree. Yet before Bitsy could ask for help from her friend, Beatrice could be heard singing...

> Good morning, good morning, good morning, I'd love to talk to you.
> But I have so very many things that I have to do.
> I wish I could stay and help you, with your wing my friend.
> But I must make some honey before this day should end.

And so Beatrice, the very busy bee, left for home. By the time she got back to her bee hive, Beatrice was not feeling too well. In fact, she was coughing and sneezing and she could tell she had a fever. As she flittered into her bed, she sang softly...

Oh me, oh my, what shall I do?
Oh me, I think I have the flu.
No friend to chat with, no carrot stew.
No one to help, what shall I do?

Beatrice drifted off to sleep that night and had a dream. She dreamed about helping her friends in their time of need and how they would be with her also, in hers.

In the morning, she awoke feeling much better. But when Beatrice got out of bed, she had very different plans for her day than she usually did. She raced out of her hive and headed straight for the nook in the forest where all her friends played together.

When she arrived and saw her friends, she began singing as loud as a little bee could sing...

Good morning, good morning, good morning, I'd love to talk to you.
I'd like to tell you I'm sorry, please know that this is true.
You are such very good friends to me, I just can't tell you how.
So I want to be a good friend to you, and I'm going to start right now.

And from that day on, Beatrice the very busy bee, started spending her time being the best friend she could be to all the forest animals.

If a Carrot and a Lettuce Raced...

Duc Nguyen

Once a carrot lived next to a lettuce.

The carrot really liked himself. He used to go over the lettuce's house all the time just to brag. He'd tell that lettuce, "Look at me, Lettuce. I'm firm, trim and filled with Vitamin A. And of course, I am the fastest veggie you'll ever meet, you big round ball of leaves!"

Well, nobody, not even a lettuce, likes to be called a big round ball of leaves day after day. Even if that is what they are. So, one day the lettuce got mad and told the carrot, "I'm tired of you, Carrot! You aren't so hot."

"My, my, isn't someone green with envy!" replied the arrogant orange carrot.

"I'm not envious, and you're not so great," blurted the lettuce. "In fact, I challenge you to a race. A race from the top of Mt. Salad down to the Juice Bar in the town square."

"You're on," crowed the carrot, "but be warned, I'm going to make salad out of you!"

The next day a crowd of veggies gathered at the top of Mt. Salad. There were tomatoes, cucumbers, onions and radishes, just to name a few. An apple from a neighboring town even showed up. No one gave the lettuce much of a chance.

But the lettuce didn't look worried. In fact, he was smiling and relaxed. He didn't even notice the carrot showing off his new running shoes.

Then it was time for the race to begin. The carrot and the lettuce stepped up to the starting line. "You won't be fit for rabbit food when I'm done with you," sneered the carrot.

"We'll see," smiled the lettuce.

Then suddenly, "Crack!" the starting gun went off.

The carrot bolted from the line. His legs pumped and pumped. His little green leaves fluttered in the air. And the lettuce? The lettuce stood patiently at the starting line.

The vegetables were aghast! What was the lettuce doing? Was he letting the carrot win?

Suddenly, the lettuce moved from the line. But he didn't start to run. No, quite the opposite. He lay down and then he began to roll. Down Mt. Salad rolled the lettuce. Faster and faster he went, building up speed. Within seconds he blew by the carrot! Whooosh!

The carrot was stunned, to say the least. He ran harder to try and catch the blazing lettuce. But the faster he ran, the farther away the lettuce was. By the time he reached the finish line, heaving and panting, the lettuce was already celebrating with the vegetables of the town.

"It's not fair," cried the carrot, "you cheated!"

"I didn't cheat," responded the lettuce, all cool and crisp. "You see, I may not be slim and trim like you. Or even be filled with Vitamin A. But the plain fact of the matter is, no matter what the race, no matter who the opponent, a lettuce will always win. Because a lettuce will always be— a-head!"

Big Wheel Cookies
by Kathy Culmer

Our house was two doors down from Simmon's Grocery Store. People in the neighborhood liked to gather at Simmons' Grocery. Sometimes the men, passing by on·their way home from work, would stop by for a 10 cent bottle of ice-cold Coca Cola out of the red and white drink box that sat behind the door. Ladies liked to get caught up with the latest happenings in the neighborhood. Children liked to hide behind the store and do lots of things.

On the counter inside the store, there were four big, round plastic containers filled with cookies— oatmeal, ginger, coconut, and Big Wheels. The others cost a penny-a-piece, but you could get two of the Big Wheel cookies— those big, round, thin butter cookies, with different faces on them— for just one penny!

Sometimes I would stand on the dirt sidewalk in front of our house, smiling at the people as they walked by, and sometimes they would give me cookies. Mr. Red McDay spent most days loading heavy furniture onto the trucks of Goode Nichols Furniture Store. "How you doin' today, girl?" he asked me, as he headed towards the store.

"All right. How are you?" I answered with a great big smile.

On his way back out he handed me a little brown paper sack, all folded up.
"Here, baby," he said, "Here's somethin' for ya. You be good."

"Thank you, Mr. Red," I answered, grinning. I opened up the bag and, there inside, I found two Big Wheel Cookies– one with a smiley-faced clown on it, and another with a picture of a little boy on a tricycle. I ran inside to the kitchen and started a stack. One... two cookies on my mama's kitchen table.

"How you today, Mr. Sims?" I called out to the old man coming slowly across the street towards me.

"Very well," he answered, throwing his hand up in the air to wave.

Mr. Barrett Sims, the older man who lived alone in the house across the street from us, stopped on his way back from the store. "Here, child. Don't eat these fo' supper. You be good, now," he added, patting me on the shoulder. He moseyed on back across the street and up the little hill that led to his front porch.

Three... four... five... six cookies on my mama's kitchen table. I barely made it back to my

spot before Mr. Joe Zellner came by, grinning from ear to ear, wearing his usual half-clean clothes and thick rubber boots.

"How'd do, little girl?" he asked, as he briskly approached.

"All right. How you?" I answered, trying to match him with my smile.

Mr. Joe stopped, looked down with his eyes peeping out from under the flap of that old cap he always wore. "Hyeah's sumthin' fur ya, li'l girl. You be good, ya hear."

"I will, Mr. Joe. Thank you."

Wow! Seven... eight Big Wheel cookies on my mama's kitchen table. I started to eat one of those cookies— just one. "Naw, maybe later," I thought to myself. But I didn't eat those cookies, not even after dinner. I never did. There was just something about having somebody give me something that made me feel good, special. It said to me, "You're okay, child, and here's something to prove you are. I don't have much to give you, maybe not even the words to say you're okay, but, today I got a penny or two extra in my pocket..."

Escape from Cambodia

by Serena Chea

My father walked the water buffalo every morning. This is how he plowed the fields. My sisters worked in the rice paddy while my brother tended the cattle. My mother took the harvest to sell at the market. I was the youngest. My mother and father always told me that I was too little to help. Even though my family had to work hard, we were happy and lived peacefully.

One day, I heard fireworks outside my house. I immediately stood up to see where the sounds were coming from. Then I heard my mother yell, "The soldiers are coming! Get down! Get down!" As we scattered towards the nearest ditch, the fireworks became increasingly louder.

"We have to escape and make it to the refugee camps. We'll be safe there!" my father assured us. We walked fast, carrying as little as possible, as we followed the massive crowd.

"Will you hurry up?" my sister said, reaching towards me.

Before I grabbed her hand, I saw something sparkle. Jewels had spilled out of a jewelry bag that someone had left behind. I ran toward the bag as my sister yelled, "No, no, don't!" Excitedly, I grabbed the jewels and hid them in my pocket. I quickly ran back to hold on tightly to my sister's hand.

We walked all day until our feet became numb. We stopped on the side of the road and my father commanded, "We can't stay here. We must keep going."

I cried, "My tummy hurts, Mommy!" My mother caressed my face and said sadly, "I know, Sweetie, but we don't have any food." Then, with trembling hands, I took the jewelry bag out of my pocket and handed it to my mother. Without hesitation, she begged one passerby to exchange the jewels for a few handfuls of rice, which we devoured immediately. Our delicious meal, meager as it was, provided us enough strength to go on.

We continued our journey during the nights to hide from the soldiers. We walked through the jungle and its muddy waters. We slept on wet ground. My mother held me tight and my tummy stopped hurting.

Then the roar of an airplane, descending from above, startled me. My mother gently cradled my head in her hands. "Everything will be alright," she whispered. "They are coming to rescue us."

Today, we live in a land where fireworks light up the sky in pretty colors but cannot hurt us and where we never fear the sound of soldiers marching in the distance.

Balancing the Moon

by Eldrena Douma

At the edge of the mesa, Coyote looked for his friend's return from her journey. After a while, he saw a cloud of dust approaching. He knew it was his friend Roadrunner, because no one could kick up dust like she could.

As Roadrunner ran circles around her friend, jumping and yelling, she finally came to a stop to greet him with a hug. Roadrunner was always going somewhere, so before she left again, Coyote wanted to tell her something.

"Roadrunner, I'm so glad you have returned from your trip. I have so many things to show you," said Coyote.

"Like what?" said Roadrunner.

"Well, I've got a new song and trick that I've been working on," said Coyote.

"Well, a new song I would like to hear. But, Coyote, I am your friend. You don't have to play a trick on me."

"It's a good trick, Roadrunner, not a bad one. Why don't you meet me at the bottom of our favorite hill tonight. I'll sing you my new desert song and show you my trick."

That night, as Roadrunner approached their favorite hill, she could hear her friend Coyote singing a beautiful desert song. Coyote noticed her coming and ran down to greet her. He took her to the perfect spot at the bottom of the hill. Then, he told her to close her eyes until he gave her the signal. Coyote then ran to the top of the hill, just as the moon was entering the sky. He waited for the moon to get in the sky right where he had measured it in his mind.

At that moment, Coyote lifted his head and howled, "LOOOOK!"

When Roadrunner opened her eyes, she couldn't believe it. Coyote was balancing the moon on his nose as he sang his new desert song.

This went on for several moments. Then Roadrunner yelled up to Coyote, saying he'd better let Moon continue it's journey across the sky. Coyote thought that was a good idea so he sent Moon on its way.

"What a wonderful trick, Coyote. You are so full of surprises. That's what I like about you. There's never a dull moment in our friendship."

That event took place a long time ago. The coyotes today can still sing desert songs, but none have mastered the trick of balancing the moon on their nose. However, I hear that some have been seen trying.

Weeping Willow

by Setha Kang

Long ago, in the middle of an island, there lived the very first Willow tree. She stood proud and tall. Her beautiful emerald leaves covered the entire island, and her shiny gold branches touched the sky. In spring, she showered the island with her seeds. In summer, she shaded her seeds from the harsh sun's rays. In fall, she fed them rain drops from heavy showers. In winter, she covered them from fearsome winter storms. The young willows grew strong and tall under her watchful care. For many years, the Willow continued to nurture and protect her children. She taught them to stand proud and always reach for the sky.

One day, a ship sailed by. Captivated by her beauty, the captain desired to make the tree his own. He halted the ship and a sea of a hundred men raced ashore, surrounding the great Willow. As they gazed upward at her mighty trunk piercing the clouds above, their hearts filled with awe. But the Captain was not a man of good faith. He commanded his men to cut the Willow down! And so, his hundred men brought forth a hundred silver axes and swung with all of their strength. Into the mighty Willow fell the sharpened blades! They pierced her thick trunk time and time again. Still, the mighty Willow stood tall, with her outstretched arms raised higher than ever!

Many sunsets passed. The men lay worn beneath the Willow's sheltering branches, their broken axes scattered across the island's shore. The dark Captain fumed. "Back to the ship!" he ordered his men. As they returned, he ordered that each man take two of the Willow's offspring, for he could surely trade such fine trees for gold! And so, the men ripped the young willows from their roots until none were left. Onto the ship the men loaded the young willow trees and they sailed away.

When their task was complete, the crater-filled island was left empty and torn apart. All that remained was a sad, weeping mother Willow. Her branches drooped to the ground, waving with the wind. Never again did the Willow touch the sky. And never to this day, have any of her children.

Every now and then, when the wind blows, we can witness one reaching towards its mother... never forgetting the time when they once stood proud and tall.

About the Authors & Illustrators

The common thread which holds together this cast of writers and illustrators is their love for stories. All are storytellers in their own right: some professionally, some through their written words, and some through the stroke of the paintbrush. Nonetheless, all contributors add a personal touch to this book, to relay their own visions and insights to the world, in a truly unique and individual fashion.

In the next few pages, you will get to know the writers and illustrators themselves: their interests, their backgrounds, and even how to contact some of them. Make a friend through sharing their stories or their art or even by getting to know them personally. And now, introducing:

the CAST...

Eric A. Kimmel is the award winning author of over forty books for children. He travels throughout the United States, speaking at schools, libraries, and conferences. His best known book, *Hershel and the Hanukkah Goblins*, was a 1990 Caldecott Honor Book. Amidst all his success, Eric is still one of the most genuine and kindest people you could ever meet. Thank you, Eric, for your generosity in making this book project possible. —VK & Friends

Brekka Hervey has been writing poetry and short stories since she was in the second grade. Every Christmas, she packages all her creative writing from that year to give as a gift to her grandmother. This tradition in her family has been alive for over 20 years. Brekka is a middle school and elementary school Language Arts teacher. She lives in Houston with her husband and their three dogs. To contact Brekka, you may find her at (713)660-8873 or e-mail her: i000smiles@aol.com

Lisa Jastram grew up in Japan as a missionary's daughter. She returned to Minnesota to attend Gustavus Adolphus College where she received her B.A. in music education. She spent several years teaching in the public schools before choosing to stay home with her two sons. In 1989, she co-founded Oasis for Children to provide educational entertainment in public schools. Lisa is a singer, composer, and performer and has written and produced three full-length musicals and released five recordings of children's music. To contact Lisa, call (281)980-8537.

Kendall Seuser was born in Dodge City, Kansas, but raised in Texas. He spent summers on his grandmother's farm in Bison, Kansas and the school year with his family in Copperas Cove, Texas. Kendall is one of seven children, so after supper, singing and storytelling was a way of life. Today, Kendall enjoys singing and performing for children all over Texas. When not working, Kendall spends time with his two sons, Grant and Stinson, telling them stories, helping them with their homework, and cooking them supper. Kendall may be reached at (713)666-7369.

Lucas Miller spent his childhood ankle-deep in a creek searching for frogs, turtles and other critters. In college, he studied zoology by day and strummed guitar in a rock band by night. These days, Lucas travels the country with a collection of environmental stories and animal songs teaching people the importance of nature. To hear his stories and songs about anacondas, skunks, fire ants, and many other creatures, call Lucas Miller at (800) 755-4415 and invite him to your school or festival.

Sherry Pearson fell in love with words as a child. A native Texan, Sherry attended the University of Houston. She was "Poet in the Schools" for Conroe ISD where she taught poetry interpretation and writing to elementary through high school students. In 1982, Sherry co-authored *Premature Babies, A Handbook for Parents* (Arbor House). She and artist George Bevill teamed up 12 years ago to create Illustrated Storytelling. She is the proud mother of three handsome sons. Sherry Pearson can be reached at (409)231-3430.

Deanna Reese Gonzales has loved reading and writing children's stories since she was a child growing up in Beaumont, Texas. Her passion for writing has continued throughout the years and she has stressed the importance of literacy to her children, who are also avid readers and creative writers. Deanna resides in Pearland, Texas with her husband Donnie and their two children, Chelsie and Joshua. She has home-schooled her children for the past six years.

Besides writing his first book *The Rolling Stone & Other Read-Aloud Stories*, **Duc Nguyen** is also working on his second book, *Elmer the Dog*. Originally from Houston, Texas, Duc has been working for the last five years in San Francisco and New York as an advertising copywriter. He also has written for a professional New York comedy troupe. Duc will begin touring for his upcoming book project in Spring 2000. To arrange an appearance, contact him at (718)768-3765 or (713)572-9822.

Kathy Hood Culmer, (storyteller, teacher, and writer) is a native of Griffin, Georgia. Kathy's experience as a teller includes solo performances as well as ensemble performances, having performed for several years with the music-telling group, Tales & Scales. Her repertoire includes folktales, sacred stories, and historical works. The two historical story-performances she is currently offering are "They Called Her Madam" and "The Little Light of Mine: the Story of Select Women in the Civil Rights Movement." E-mail: khculmer@aol.com

Born in Battambang, Cambodia in 1970, **Serena Ravy Chea** arrived in the United States in 1981. She graduated from the University of Texas in Austin in 1996 and received a Bachelor of Science in Medical Technology. She is married and has three brothers and three sisters. She also has two chihuahuas named Picasso and Rocky. She credits her parents as her inspirations in life. She lives in Houston and can be contacted at (281)880-9501.

Eldrena Douma, a professional storyteller, travels throughout the United States sharing stories from her American Indian background. She presents workshops on creative writing and storytelling. Her experience as a storyteller began as a child listening to family and friends tell stories about life experiences, history, and folktales. Today, Eldrena continues to develop stories of her own unique creation, full of rich heritage and tradition. She is the founder and president of Storytellers of the High Plains. For visits, call (806)655-0675.

Setha Kang was born in Cambodia and immigrated to the United States in 1975. She grew up in Los Angeles, California, and currently resides in Houston. This is her first book which she dedicates to her mom and dad, her brother Vathana, her new niece Jocelyn, and her little brother Vaughn. She wishes to thank her family for their infinite love and support and her friends for all of their encouragement. She would especially like to thank Vuthy Kuon and the Goh's for being a wonderful inspiration. Phone: (713)290-9923 (for school visits)

Vuthy Kuon (right) and **Dez Tyler** (left) became friends through their passion for art. This illustration is their first of many collaborative pieces. Vuthy (pronounced WOOD-TEE) has illustrated 4 other children's books, most notably, *Humpty Dumpty After the Fall*. Dez is most known for his graffiti art and comic books, but also does contemporary clothing design. Both Vuthy and Dez are available for illustration projects and school visits or just to talk and make new friends. To contact them, you may call (888)966-3833 or e-mail at woodtee@aol.com

Never far from a pencil and crayons, **Steve O'Shea** grew up in the desert of eastern Washington where he spent many a blissful hour drawing space ships, fast cars, and cowboys. These efforts blossomed into a dual career in architecture and illustration, where Steve has been designing buildings and creating bright whimsical illustrations for clients throughout the West and beyond. Steve lives in Portland, Oregon where he lives with his wife, Jan, and children, Daniel and Caitlin. Steve can be reached at sodraw@transport.com or (503) 520-0850.

Kevin Ryan, graduated from the University of Houston with a degree in Graphic Design. His illustration work has been featured on various covers of the Star Wars comic book series, commissioned by Lucasfilm/ Dark Horse Comics. Kevin's work as a muralist can also be seen in many Houston-based business and homes, including Loews/Sony Theatres. He can be contacted for illustration projects at (281)873-6603 or via e-mail: kryan@texas.net

Jarrett J. Krosoczka grew up in Worcester, Massachusetts. He would later receive his BFA in Illustration from the Rhode Island School of Design. He has illustrated reading books for McGraw Hill. Jarrett is actively involved in Camp Sunshine and The Hole in the Wall Gang Camp, camps for children with life threatening illnesses or disorders. He currently resides outside Boston where he freelance, illustrates, and writes for children's books.   E-mail: Jarrett77@aol.com
Website: http://members.aol.com/Jarrett77/illustration.html

Brady Smith began drawing at a very early age. His father would often work at a drafting table and Brady would sit on top of the desk, drawing like his dad. He showed an incredible talent, even at the age of three. Brady received a Bachelor of Fine Arts with an emphasis in advertising design from Stephen F. Austin State University. He also spends his time volunteering for the Lighthouse of Houston, an organization dedicated to assisting blind and the visually impaired. You can find him on-line at www.bradysmith.com or call (713)752-6572.

George Bevill began his formal training in Louisiana College. As a watercolorist, Mr. Bevill has won numerous local and national awards. He is known for his landscapes, murals, magazine covers and portraits of notable politicians and sports figures. For the past twelve years, George has partnered with Mrs. Sherry Pearson to make the Illustrated Storytelling team. Travelling throughout Texas and surrounding states, he makes her stories come to visual life with the use of chalk drawing and the magic of florescent lighting.

Beatrice Baldwin hold degrees in art from the University of Colorado and the University of North Texas. She has illustrated a calendar for children called "Mouse Months" and a variation of the "The Little Red Hen." She lives in Chatham, Virginia with her white labrador retriever, Sugar.
E-mail: summergatebea@hotmail.com
Address: PO Box 235, 800 Chatham Hall Circle, Chatham, VA 24531
Phone: (804)432-8980

Grace Lin graduated from Rhode Island School of Design and now works as a freelance illustrator. Her illustrations have appeared in publications such as Weekly Reader, Seventeen, and Girl's Life Magazine. Grace is the author of *The Ugly Vegetables* (Charlesbridge / 1999) as well as the illustrator of *The Big Buck Adventure* (Charlesbridge / 2000) and *Round is a Mooncake* (Chronicle / 2000). Grace lives in Cambridge, Massachusetts in a bright yellow room. Contact her at (617)629-7735
E-mail: gracelin@concentric.net   Website: www.chris.com/gracelin

Lori Loebelsohn grew up in Brooklyn, New York. She graduated from the Cooper Union and has a master's degree in education from Hunter's College. Mrs. Loebelsohn works as a freelance illustrator. Her clients include Harper-Collins, Cambridge University Press, and the Lefferts Homestead Children's Museum. She loves to paint children and has recently completed a series of children's portraits. She currently lives with her husband and two children in New Jersey. For illustration projects, Lori can be contacted at (973) 566-0380.

Jamie Assad, an atypical graduate of Rhode Island School of Design, finds herself strangely at home in the murky waters of Galveston Bay. Despite her sophisticated cultural upbringing, her lifelong dream is to rule the ocean as a world renowned fishing boat captain. In the meantime, she fills her days with golfing, hunting, and a little bit of painting. This native Texan accredits all of her impressive pieces of art to her best friend, Jesus Christ... all of her non-impressive pieces are her own fault. E-mail: Jim1963@texas.net

Karen E. Bessette graduated from the Rhode Island School of Design in 1996 with a BFA in Illustration. Karen has exhibited in several shows and galleries within New Hampshire and Rhode Island. Using bright vivid colors and textures through collage, she adds a lively quality to her images. This is Karen's first book and she looks forward to creating more of her whimsical illustrations for publication. She works as a freelance illustrator in Manchester, New Hampshire. Phone: (603)623-1749   E-mail: bantail@aol.com

Brad Gaber received his BFA from the University of Texas in Austin. He then studied with Milton Glaser at the School of Visual Art in New York City. Back in Houston, he continued his freelance career in earnest with fortune 500 companies and major ad agencies as his clientele. In 1979, Gaber helped to found the Houston Society of Illustrators with a dozen of his colleagues. He has also served on the boards of the Art Directors Club of Houston and several public service agencies. To contact Brad for freelance projects, please call (713)723-0300.